For Charles and Annabel, the most excellent audience . . .
—D.T.

To Max, Andre and Lena
—B.K.

Text copyright © 2010 by David Teague · Illustrations copyright © 2010 by Boris Kulikov
All rights reserved. · Published by Disney • Hyperion Books, an imprint of Disney Book Group.
No part of this book may be reproduced or transmitted in any form or by any means, electronic or mechanical,
including photocopying, recording, or by any information storage and retrieval system, without written
permission from the publisher. For information address Disney • Hyperion Books,
114 Fifth Avenue, New York, New York 10011-5690.
Printed in Singapore · First Edition · 1 3 5 7 9 10 8 6 4 2
F850-6835-5-10121 · This book is set in Adobe Garamond.
Designed by Elizabeth H. Clark · Reinforced binding
Library of Congress Cataloging-in-Publication Data on file.
ISBN 978-1-4231-1919-7 · Visit www.hyperionbooksforchildren.com

FRANKLIN'S BIG DREAMS

STORY BY
David Teague • PICTURES BY
Boris Kulikov

DISNEY • HYPERION BOOKS
NEW YORK

One night,
while he was staring at the moon, wishing he could visit it,
Franklin heard somebody tapping on his wall.

Only it wasn't exactly tapping. It was more like . . .

"What are you doing?"

said Franklin to the man with the sledgehammer.

"You're supposed to be asleep!" exclaimed the man.

"Maybe I *would* be asleep," said Franklin, "if you hadn't busted through my wall."

The man looked perturbed. He scratched his head. He checked his watch. He looked at his plans. "Are you going to sleep anytime soon?" he asked.

"I don't think so," said Franklin.

"Well, I haven't got all night," said the man. "Comin' through!"

"Through my bedroom?" asked Franklin.

"Yep," said the man. "Watch your elbows."

Franklin heard a lonesome whistle.
A light glowed in the distance.

A colossal silver train thundered through his bedroom.

As its windows flickered past, Franklin recognized the checkout lady from the grocery store, the mailman, and his dentist.

And in the last window of the final car, Franklin saw the back of a little boy's head.

Something about it seemed familiar.

Franklin wished he could've ridden that train.

After the train's lights faded, Franklin heard more noise.

It was the man with the sledgehammer again. "We have to take down the railroad," he announced.

"Why?" asked Franklin.

The man checked his plans. He said, "Everybody got where they needed to go."

After the railroad was gone, Franklin felt lonely.

He went to sleep, and dreamed he was rushing through moonlight while forests and houses streamed past him.

Things were quiet for about a week,

but then, the following Tuesday, Franklin heard a scratching on the roof.

Only it wasn't exactly scratching. It was more like . . .

"What are you doing?" Franklin asked the man with the buzz saw.

"Awake again?" asked the man.

"Well, you just buzz-sawed through my roof," Franklin answered.

The man looked miffed. He rubbed his nose. He checked his watch, and he looked at his plans. "I guess you're not going to sleep anytime soon?" he said.

"Nope," replied Franklin.

"Well, I haven't got all night," said the man. "I'm comin' through!"

"Again?" asked Franklin.

"Just keep your head down," said the man.

Franklin heard a roaring noise.

A light glowed in the distance.

A colossal jet came screaming out of the shrubbery.

Just as it got to Franklin's bedroom, it took off.

As the jet's little oval windows flickered overhead, Franklin saw the security guard from the bank, his piano teacher, and Uncle Marty.

And in the very last window, there was that little boy's head. Franklin thought possibly he recognized the cowlick.

As the plane rose into the evening sky, Franklin wished he could go along.

After the roar died down, Franklin heard another noise.

It was the man with the buzz saw. "We have to rip up the runway," he said.

"Everybody got where they needed to go?" asked Franklin.

The man checked his plans. "Looks that way," he said.

After the man and his crew left, Franklin felt lonely.

He went to sleep and dreamed that he flew so high,
he found twelve new stars.

Things were quiet at Franklin's house for a while,

but then, one Thursday night, a rumbling came through the floor.
Only it wasn't exactly rumbling. It was more like . . .

"Now what?" Franklin asked the man with the jackhammer.

"Canal—" said the man.

"Through my bedroom." Franklin nodded.

"How'd you guess?" the man said. "Tuck in your toes."

Franklin felt a powerful vibration.

A light glowed in the distance.

An ocean liner came steaming up the canal.

Waving at him over the rail were his mother's boss, the school bus driver, and the guy from across the street who wore Hawaiian shirts even in December.

"Have fun in Oahu!" Franklin shouted.

"Thanks," yelled the guy.

Leaning against the bow rail was a kid whose ears stuck out in a memorable way.

As the ocean liner disappeared into the distance, Franklin wished he was on it.

After the vibration of the engine faded, Franklin heard another noise.

It was the man with the jackhammer. "We have to fill in the canal," he said.

"Okay," sighed Franklin. "Fine."

Franklin felt lonely when they were done.

But after a while, he fell asleep and dreamed of seas no one had ever seen.

The next morning,

Franklin woke with a start. "Wait a second," he said.

    He ran to the bathroom and checked out the back of his head in the mirror. "Aha!"

When the man returned,

the moon was full outside Franklin's window.

"I figured out what's going on," said Franklin.

"Nobody knows how this works," the man said.

"Well, I do," said Franklin, "and there's a place I've always wanted to go."

"Okay," sighed the man. "But you've got to keep quiet."

"I can do that."